Pokémon®
Challenge

by Tracey West
and Katherine Nolls

SCHOLASTIC INC.

New York   Toronto   London   Auckland   Sydney

Mexico City   New Delhi   Hong Kong   Buenos Aires

ISBN-13: 978-0-439-53052-1
ISBN-10: 0-439-53052-0

12 11 10 9 8 7 6 5 4 3   8 9 10 11 12/0

Printed in the U.S.A.
First printing, March 2003

Table of Contents

Take the Challenge
A Word from Professor Oak

The world of Pokémon is filled with all kinds of puzzles. Why does Pikachu's electric power pack so much punch? Why does HootHoot only stand on one foot? And will Team Rocket ever win at anything?

As a Pokémon researcher, I study puzzles like this every day. Now it's your turn. Inside these pages you'll find plenty of **puzzles**, along with **secret messages**, **mysteries**, and **more**!

You can solve the puzzles just for fun — or use them to test your skills as a Pokémon expert. Each challenge allows you to earn Poké Points.

Look for this symbol to see how many total points you have a chance to earn each time. Finish the puzzle, then check your answers in the back of the book to see how many points you've earned.

When you've completed this book, add up all of your points. Then check the scoring chart on page 58 to find out if you are an expert at solving puzzles — or just washed up.

Best of luck, Pokémon trainer! And if these puzzles leave you puzzled, don't despair. Just relax and have fun! That's one of the best things about being a Pokémon expert.

Memory Test 1

Carefully study this picture of Team Rocket for ten seconds. (Ask a friend to count for you.) Then turn the page and put your memory to the test by answering questions about the picture. And remember, no peeking! That would be cheating, and unless you are a member of Team Rocket, you don't want to do it!

Poké Points: **for each correct answer**

1. How many people are in the picture?

   _____

2. How many Pokémon are pictured?

   _____

3. What Pokémon has both feet off the floor?

   _____

4. What Pokémon has one foot off the floor?

   _____

5. Is Jessie kneeling on one knee?

   _____

6. What Pokémon is next to Jessie?

   _____

7. Which person is next to Meowth?

   _____

8. What letter is on Jessie's and James's shirts?

   _____

Misty's Grid

Misty went on a walk and spotted two Pokémon. The names of the Pokémon are hiding in the grid below. Follow the instructions to cross out letters in the grid. The remaining letters will spell the names of the Pokémon.

1. Cross out the letters in Misty's name.
2. Cross out any letters found in this person's name.
3. Cross out all of the letters in column 3.

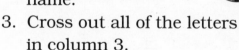

```
A K U M S E Y I
S C B Y L T I M
T A F E H O S N
W O Q M O H P I
S M J E A R Y H
```

_____ and _____

Poké Points: **for each correct answer**

Battle Busters 1

In a Pokémon battle, a trainer never knows what move another trainer will make next. A good Pokémon trainer needs to know about all different kinds of Pokémon.

In each of the battles below, imagine that all of the Pokémon are the same level. Then pick the Pokémon you think will beat your opponent's Pokémon.

1. Your opponent throws a Poké Ball, and a Crobat comes flying out. Which of these Pokémon do you think can beat it?

    a. Machamp
    b. Spinarak
    c. Raikou

Poké Points: **for each correct answer**

2. A cute little Hoppip pops out of your opponent's Poké Ball. What Pokémon will you choose?

a. Slugma
b. Totodile
c. Sentret

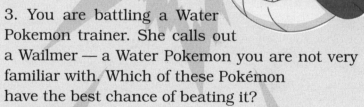

3. You are battling a Water Pokemon trainer. She calls out a Wailmer — a Water Pokemon you are not very familiar with. Which of these Pokémon have the best chance of beating it?

a. Gligar
b. Geodude
c. Pichu

4. How sweet! A smiling Blissey is ready to battle. Even though it's so happy, you still want to beat it. Which Pokémon can do the job?
   a. Marill
   b. Sudowoodo
   c. Teddiursa

5. A Donphan is rolling right toward you! Pick a Pokémon to defeat it.
   a. Mareep
   b. Azurill
   c. Voltorb

6. You are having a friendly battle with a trainer who calls on a Sunflora. Which of your Pokémon will defeat this Grass Pokémon?
   a. Typhlosion
   b. Remoraid
   c. Sandshrew

7. A sizzling hot Magcargo comes slithering out of your opponent's Poké Ball. Which of these Pokémon can beat it?

  a. Elekid
  b. Bulbasaur
  c. Feraligatr

8. Team Rocket's at it again! They want to fight you with their Wobbuffet. Which Pokémon will you choose to fight back with?

  a. Scizor
  b. Jigglypuff
  c. Rattata

Movie Moment

In *Pokémon 4Ever, Voice of the Forest,* Ash actually gets to fly — thanks to the amazing powers of Celebi.

Ears to You!

Can you identify these Pokémon by looking at their ears? All of these ears belong to the Pokémon listed below. See if you can figure out which ear belongs to which Pokémon.

Aipom   Ampharos   Azurill   Elekid   Furret
Girafarig   Gligar   Hoppip   Teddiursa   Umbreon

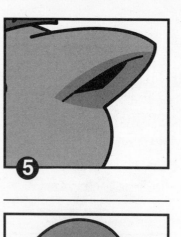

5

6

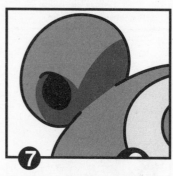

7

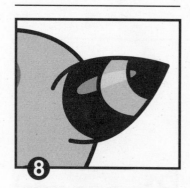

8

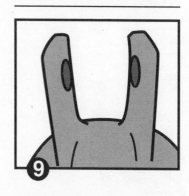

9

10

Poké Points: for each correct answer

Logic Puzzle 1

Ash, Misty, Brock, and their friend, Tracey Sketchitt, took a day off of Pokémon training to go to a carnival. Each one of them won a prize — a stuffed Pokémon doll. Here are the dolls they won:

Which friend won which doll? To figure it out, study the clues below.

1. Misty and Tracey won Water Pokémon dolls.
2. Ash won a doll with wings.
3. Tracey's Pokémon doll is green.

Can you guess which Pokémon doll each trainer won? Write your answers here:

1. Ash won _____

2. Misty won _____

3. Brock won _____

4. Tracey won _____

Poké Points: **10** total

Movie Moment

In *Pokémon the First Movie: Mewtwo Strikes Back*, legendary Pokémon Mew awoke from its sleep in the ocean to face off against its clone, Mewtwo. To this day, Pokémon experts argue about which Pokémon is stronger!

Electric Pokémon Search

Pikachu is one of the cutest Pokémon around, but its electric attacks are packed with power! The Pokémon universe is filled with Pokémon that boast sizzling abilities. See how many names of Electric Pokémon you can find and circle in this word search puzzle. The names can go up, down, left, right, backward, and diagonally. Shock your friends by finding all 14 names!

Poké Points: **1** **for each Pokémon you find**

Name Box

Magneton	Elekid	Electabuzz
Flaafy	Voltorb	Raichu
Lanturn	Mareep	Zapdos
Ampharos	Jolteon	Raikou
Electrode	Pichu	

```
U  M  A  G  N  E  T  O  N  M
Z  Y  F  A  A  L  F  U  O  P
A  N  P  I  C  E  H  X  E  I
M  R  S  H  O  C  K  E  T  B
P  U  A  A  I  T  R  P  L  R
H  T  E  A  U  A  P  D  O  O
A  N  R  B  M  B  I  I  J  T
R  A  I  K  O  U  C  K  B  L
O  L  Z  A  P  Z  H  E  U  O
S  O  D  P  A  Z  U  L  Z  V
Z  E  D  O  R  T  C  E  L  E
```

Mini-Mystery 1

Ash and his friends have solved some Pokémon mysteries during their travels. See if you can match wits with Ash and be a Pokémon detective too!

Case of the Pretty Pokémon Potion

Ash, Misty, and Brock were relaxing in a park on a sunny day with their Pokémon. Ash noticed a girl walking by. Behind her were two fiery Slugma.

"Hi there. I'm Ash," Ash said. "You must really like Slugma."

"Hi, I'm Amy," said the girl. "I love Slugma! They are my favorite Pokémon."

"They move so slow," said Brock. "Isn't it hard to travel with them?"

"If I need to move fast, I just put them in their Poké Balls," she said. "But Slugma always need to keep moving. If they stop, even to sleep, the poor things would cool off and harden up. Then they couldn't move at all!"

Just then, three people walked to the center of the park and set up a platform. Two of the people were tall and one was very short. They all wore white lab coats and glasses.

"Attention!" one of the taller people called out. "We are scientists who have developed an amazing product. Presenting Pretty Pokémon Potion! It can make all Pokémon more beautiful."

"All you have to do is give your Pokémon the potion at night," said the other scientist. "It will wake up beautiful!"

"*Meo* — I mean, that's right!" said the short scientist.

The first scientist pointed at Amy. "We tested our potion on a Slugma. We gave it two tablespoons before bed. It slept all night, and when it woke up, it was the most beautiful shade of orange. It won a Pokémon beauty contest."

Everyone in the park crowded around the platform. They all wanted to buy the potion.

"Hold it right there!" cried Ash. "Don't waste your money. The Pretty Pokémon Potion is a fake!"

How does Ash know the potion won't work? Turn to the answer key to find out.

Secret Message 1

Won't Team Rocket ever learn? They crashed a Prize Pokémon Show and sent a message to their boss, Giovanni, telling him what they planned to steal. The message is in code, but when Ash saw it he realized that if he took the first letter of each Pokémon's name he could spell words. Can you help Ash decode this secret message? Write the first letter of each Pokémon's name above its picture.

Poké Points: **total**

_____ _____

_____ _____ _____ _____

_____ _____ _____

_____ _____ _____ _____

_____ _____ _____

_____ _____ _____ _____ _____ _____

Hidden Name Challenge

Kecleon is a new Pokémon with the ability to camouflage itself. That means it can change color to blend in to any setting. In this challenge, you'll find the names of twelve Pokémon camouflaged in the sentences below. Each sentence contains one hidden name. The first one has been done to get you started.

1. Co**me w**ith me.

_____

2. The shop piped music over a loudspeaker.

_____

3. Mom served me a good dish of ice cream.

_____

4. I've got to get ice for my water.

_____

5. The white lab rats chattered in their cage.

_____

6. Please get the horse a drink.

_____

Poké Points: 2 **total**

7. Do you see lights over there?

_____

8. This new cleaner gets grime right off!

_____

9. It is fun owning a bike.

_____

10. Michele kids around a lot.

_____

11. Most mice fear owls.

_____

12. Close the window or else a draft will get in.

_____

Movie Moment

In the movie short _Pikachu and Pichu in the City_, Pikachu meets the adorable — and mischievous — Pichu twins for the first time. Here's a tip for telling the twins apart: one has a tuft of hair on top of its head.

Amazing Anagrams

An anagram is what you get when you take one word and rearrange it to make one or more new words. If you take the letters in WAILMER, for example, you can make RAW LIME, WARM LIE.

Got it? Good. On these pages you'll find anagrams made from the names of Pokémon. Using the clues, rearrange the letters in the words to spell the Pokémon names.

1. Clue: Red and black Bug Pokémon.
   LINE AD

   _____

2. Clue: Tougher than Snubbull.
   BALL RUNG

   _____

3. Clue: Looks like a pretty flower.
   BLOOM LESS

   _____

Poké Points: **1** **for each correct answer**

22

4. Clue: Psychic Pokémon with a pendant.
PHONY

_____

5. Clue: Hangs out with Remoraid.
ANT MINE

_____

6. Clue: A member of Team Rocket.
THE MOW

_____

7. Clue: Looks like a walking ball of noodles.
LEAN TAG

_____

8. Clue: Related to Zubat.
RAT COB

_____

9. Clue: Can stand up straight on its tail.
NET REST

_____

10. Clue: Its wings look like steel.
ROY MARKS

_____

23

Nurse Joy's Grid

Two nervous Pokémon have escaped from the Pokémon Center. Can you help Nurse Joy find them in the grid? Follow the instructions below to cross out letters in the grid. The remaining letters will spell their names.

1. Cross out any letters that appear in this Pokémon's name.

2. Cross out the letter "J" for Joy.

3. X out the letter "X."

B S O A M X Y H

S L C J E O E O

F J G X I H R J

A O F U A J M J

M R J I X C U G

_ _ _ _ _ _ _ _ **and** _ _ _ _ _ _ _ _

Memory Test 2

Study this picture of Ash and his Pokémon for ten seconds. (Have someone count out the time for you.) Then turn the page and see how many questions you can answer correctly. Remember, no cheating!

Poké Points: 1 **for each correct answer**

1. What Pokémon is sitting on Ash's head?

_____

2. Is Bayleef jumping in the air?

_____

3. Which Pokémon is flying?

_____

4. What is Ash holding in his right hand?

_____

5. Is Totodile's mouth closed or open?

_____

6. What Pokémon is underneath Noctowl?

_____

7. Does Cyndaquil have flames coming out of its back?

_____

8. Is Ash standing still or running?

_____

Who's That Character?

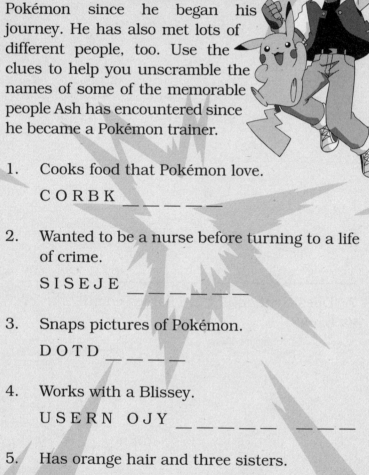

Ash has met many amazing Pokémon since he began his journey. He has also met lots of different people, too. Use the clues to help you unscramble the names of some of the memorable people Ash has encountered since he became a Pokémon trainer.

1. Cooks food that Pokémon love.

   C O R B K _ _ _ _ _

2. Wanted to be a nurse before turning to a life of crime.

   S I S E J E _ _ _ _ _ _

3. Snaps pictures of Pokémon.

   D O T D _ _ _ _

4. Works with a Blissey.

   U S E R N O J Y _ _ _ _ _ _ _ _ _

5. Has orange hair and three sisters.

   Y T M I S _ _ _ _ _

6. Comes from a rich family.

   S E M A J _ _ _ _ _

7. Takes care of Ash's Muk.

   R O S E P R F O S K A O

   _ _ _ _ _ _ _ _ _   _ _ _

8. Fights crime on a motorcycle.

   C F I O R E F N E N J Y

   _ _ _ _ _ _ _   _ _ _ _ _

9. Likes to sketch Pokémon, now helps out Professor Oak.

   Y E C A R T _ _ _ _ _ _

10. Bosses around Team Rocket.

    I I N G V N O A _ _ _ _ _ _ _ _ _

11. Runs a Charizard preserve and takes care of Ash's Charizard.

    A Z I L _ _ _ _

12. Professor Oak's Eevee-training grandson.

    Y A R G _ _ _ _

13. This boy time-traveled with Celebi in *Pokémon 4 Ever: The Voice of the Forest.*

    A M S Y M _ _ _ _ _

14. This villain makes evil Pokémon using a Dark Ball.

    N O I R S K A M

    _ _ _ _ _ _ _ _ _ _

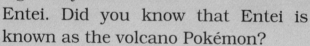

Movie Moment

In *Pokémon the Movie 3: Spell of the Unknown,* Ash's mom is carried off by the legendary Pokémon Entei. Did you know that Entei is known as the volcano Pokémon?

Battle Busters 2

Ready to battle again? Read each scenario and pick the Pokémon you think can win. Remember, all the Pokémon are the same level.

1. Your opponent gives a yell, and a Muk slithers out. Which of these Pokémon will make Muk wish it had stayed in its Poké Ball?
   a. Tangela
   b. Gligar
   c. Skiploom

2. A Yanma is flying overhead. Your opponent thinks he's got you beat. But you know you can win if you pick this Pokémon.
   a. Cyndaquil
   b. Stantler
   c. Porygon

3. Ouch! Stay away from the sharp spikes of your opponent's Water Pokémon, Qwilfish. You don't want your Pokémon to get hurt, so carefully choose which one can do the job.
   a. Larvitar
   b. Flaaffy
   c. Cyndaquil

4. When your opponent calls on the tough Entei, you get a little worried. But then you remember you have this Pokémon. Which Pokémon is as tough as Entei?

  a. Bellossom
  b. Pineco
  c. Suicune

5. Which of these Pokémon would you call on to beat the electrifying Ampharos?

  a. Snubbull
  b. Charmander
  c. Phanpy

6. A Pineco pops out of your opponent's Poké Ball. Which Pokémon can beat it?

  a. Magby
  b. Umbreon
  c. Meganium

7. To start the match, your opponent sends out a spinning Hitmontop. Which Pokemon can stop it in its tracks?

   a. Swinub
   b. Alakazam
   c. Larvitar

8. You meet a trainer who won't stop bragging about her Dratini. When she challenges you to a battle, you need to pick a Pokémon that will stop her bragging! Which one will you choose?

   a. Delibird
   b. Tangela
   c. Scizor

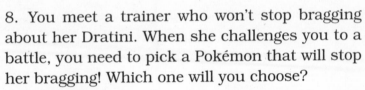

Movie Moment

   Being a Pokémon trainer is a big enough challenge. In *Pokémon the Movie 2000*, Ash discovered that he was destined to save the world!

Mini-Mystery 2

Are you ready for another mini-mystery? See if you can figure out the answer to this one.

The Case of the Cheating Trainer

Ash, Misty, and Brock journeyed to a new town and found the Pokémon gym. Ash was hoping for a battle. He saw a girl standing by the gym door.

"Hi!" Ash said. "Are you a trainer? Do you want to battle?'

"Sure," said the girl. "Sounds like fun. My name is Lauren. What's your name?"

"My name is Ash," said Ash with a smile.

"Ash Ketchum? No way would I battle a cheater like you," Lauren cried, and walked away.

"How strange," Misty said. "Why would she say something like that about you? You are no cheater!"

Lauren walked over to a boy with red hair. The two of them began to battle.

"I know that trainer!" Ash said. "I battled him two towns ago, and I won! His name is Eric."

When the battle finished, Ash approached Eric. "Nice battle," Ash said. "Do you remember me? I'm Ash Ketchum. We battled two weeks ago."

A group of trainers had crowded around to congratulate Eric. They all muttered when they heard Ash's name.

"Hey, Eric!" one of them yelled from the crowd. "Isn't this the trainer who beat you by cheating?"

Eric blushed bright red. "Well . . ." he stammered.

"I did not cheat!" Ash yelled.

"Come on," one of the trainers yelled. "Eric told us all about you and your tricks. Tell him, Eric."

Eric looked around at the crowd. Then he looked at Ash. "You did too cheat. My Feraligatr was battling against your Pikachu.

You let your Chikorita sneak behind Feraligatr and give it a Thundershock. You made me lose the match!"

"That is not true!" Ash cried. "Eric was just embarrassed to tell you all that I beat him fair and square. He is lying and I can prove it!"

How does Ash know that Eric is lying? If you think you know, turn to the answer key and find out if you are right.

Logic Puzzle 2

While on his way to a new Pokémon gym, Ash stopped at a Pokémon Center to rest and relax with his Pokémon. Pikachu, Bayleef, Totodile, Bulbasaur and Cyndaquil had a great time meeting other Pokémon there. In fact, each one made a new friend:

Each of Ash's Pokémon made a different friend. Read the four clues to figure out which Pokémon became friends?

1. Pikachu and Cyndaquil made friends with Ground-type Pokémon.

2. Totodile made friends with a Fire Pokémon.

3. Cyndaquil's friend is brown.

4. Bayleef's friend can fly.

Poké Points:  **total**

Did you figure out which Pokémon became friends? Write your answers here:

1. Pikachu became friends with

_____

2. Bayleef became friends with

_____

3. Totodile became friends with

_____

4. Bulbasaur became friends with

_____

5. Cyndaquil became friends with

_____

Movie Moment

In the movie short *Pikachu's Rescue Adventure*, Pikachu and its friends search for a runaway Togepi. They found their friend in a nest of Exeggcute.

Normal Pokémon Search

Anyone who knows Team Rocket's talking Pokémon Meowth knows that Meowth is anything but normal! But Meowth is a Normal-type Pokémon, just like many others in the Pokémon universe. They might be Normal, but these Pokémon are all very special in their own way.

Test your Poké smarts! See how many names of Normal-type Pokémon you can circle in this word search puzzle — without a name box to help you out! The names go up, down, across, from left to right, backward, and diagonally. Good luck finding all 13 of them!

```
A   S   R   U   I   D   D   E   T   S
C   S   N   O   R   L   A   X   W   E
H   P   E   R   S   I   A   N   O   N
A   A   R   D   P   C   A   T   E   T
N   Y   Z   O   C   K   T   E   S   R
S   E   M   D   N   I   A   O   M   E
E   S   W   U   D   T   R   H   C   T
Y   S   P   O   T   U   B   C   O   E
M   I   L   T   A   N   K   I   W   R
F   L   I   T   O   G   E   P   I   R
A   B   G   N   I   R   A   S   R   U
J   I   G   G   L   Y   P   U   F   F
```

Sweet Feet

Can you identify these Pokémon just by looking at their feet? All of the feet below belong to the Pokémon listed here. See if you can figure out which foot belongs to which Pokémon.

Bellsprout   Houndoom   Krabby   Murkrow   Natu   Octillery
Politoed   Shuckle   Spinarak   Sudowoodo

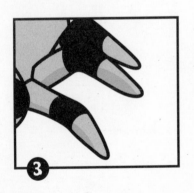

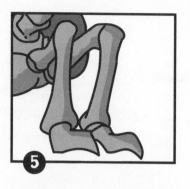

5

6

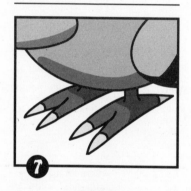

7

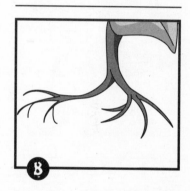

8

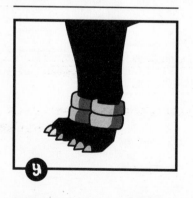

9

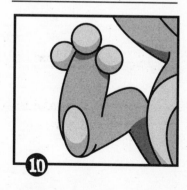

10

Poké Points: **for each correct answer**

41

Secret Message 2

In *Pokémon 4 Ever: The Voice of the Forest*, Ash encountered some amazing new Pokémon. Even Pikachu met some brand new Pokémon in *Pikachu's Pika Boo*.

Ash wants to send some information about these Pokémon to Professor Oak. He's sending it in code so Team Rocket won't intercept it. Use the key to figure out the messages.

A	B	C	D	E	F	G	H	I	J
☆	┼	❀	✛	✜	◆	◇	★	☆	✪

K	L	M	N	O	P	Q	R	S	T
☆	★	★	★	★	☆	✳	✳	✳	✳

	U	V	W	X	Y	Z			
	✳	✦	✳	✠	✸	☀			

1.

 Poké Points: **for each correct answer**

2. ☆ ✹ ✳ ✳ ☆ ★ ★ ✹ ☆ ★ ★

✢ ★ ✳ ★ ✳ ✢ ☆ ★ ★ ★ ★ ☆ ✳ ☆ ★ ★.

3. ✳ ☆ ☆ ★ ★ ✢ ✳ ☆ ✳ ☆ ✳ ★ ☆ ★ ✢

☆ ★ ☆) ★ ★ ★.

4. ☆ ✢ ✻ ★ ✢ ★ ★ ✿ ☆ ★ ✿ ★ ☆ ★ ◇ ✢

✿ ★ ★ ★ ✳.

5. ✳ ✹ ☆ ✢ ✳ ✪ ✢ ✢ ☆ ✪ ✢ ✪ ✢ ☆ ✪

☆ ★ ★ ★ ✳ ✳ ✢ ✿ ✳ ☆ ✳ ✢ ✳.

Movie Moment

In *Pikachu's Pika Boo*, Togepi gets lost on the beach and is carried away by the waves. Luckily, Wailmer rescues the little Pokémon!

Crossword Challenge

Misty's Psyduck always looks so puzzled, doesn't it? Poor Psyduck would probably never figure out this crossword puzzle. See if you can do better. Use the clues below to fill in the crossword grid on page 45.

ACROSS

1. The second evolved form of Hoppip.

4. This blue Water Pokémon has a swirl on its tummy.

7. Articuno is an ____ - type Pokémon.

8. This Normal/Flying Pokémon likes to stand on one foot.

10. This blue Water Pokémon is fond of round objects.

13. This Pokémon can evolve into Furret.

14. Some Water Pokémon, like Quagsire, have an attack called ____ Dance.

16. Some Pokémon use a Confuse ___ attack to mix up their opponents.

17. Pikachu has a black stripe on the tip of each _____.

18. Pikachu also has a red ____ on each cheek.

20. ____ upon a time, there was a Pokémon trainer named Ash.

21. Ash's Chikorita evolved into _____.

22. This new Pokémon can change color to match its surroundings.

DOWN

1. This pretty Grass Pokémon is sunny during the day, but stays perfectly still at night.

2. This little Electric Pokémon is smaller than Pikachu — and just as cute!

3. Finish this Pokémon's name: Ho-__.

4. The name of the man who gave Ash his first Pokémon.

5. This Pokémon evolves into Quagsire.

6. When Ash throws out a Poké Ball, he might yell, "___, Noctowl!"

9. Some Pokémon use their sharp teeth to deliver a attack.

10. Cyndaquil evolves into this Pokémon.

11. This Rock/Ground Pokémon looks like a boulder with big, strong arms.

12. Brock calls on this big Rock Pokémon a lot.

15. This sweet pink Pokémon is known as the Star-shape Pokémon.

18. A lovable, white Water Pokémon with a horn on his head.

19. Ash lives in Pallet ____.

21. Like the song goes: "Born to __ a winner!"

Poké Points: **for each correct answer**

 46

Mini-Mystery 3

This is your last chance to match wits with Ash and solve a mini-mystery. Look for clues in the story to help you figure out the answer.

The Case of the Stolen Pidgey Egg

Ash, Misty, and Brock decided to take a break and go to a Pidgey Festival in the park.

"The Pidgey eggs in the woods next to the park will be hatching soon," Brock said. "This should be interesting."

"But which way to the festival?" Ash asked.

Ash spotted a young boy walking with a HootHoot on his shoulder. "Hey, kid, do you know where the Pidgey festival is?"

"Sure, that's where we are heading," said the boy. "My name is Ralph, and this is my HootHoot. Why don't you walk with us?"

Ash and his friends introduced themselves. Just then, a boy and a Sneasel came running by. They bumped into Ralph and nearly knocked him over.

Poké Points:  **total**

"Are you okay?" Ash asked. "Who was that kid?"

"His name is Derek, and he's a real bully," said Ralph. "I don't know why he's taking his Sneasel to the Pidgey Festival. Everyone knows Sneasels love to eat Pidgey eggs."

Ash and his friends followed Derek to the festival. They were having fun when Officer Jenny appeared, blowing her whistle.

"One of the Pidgey nests is missing an egg! Nobody move!"

At that moment, Ralph's HootHoot hopped on one leg out of the woods carrying an egg. Derek and his Sneasel came running out after it.

"Here's your egg thief," Derek said. "We followed a pair of footprints to a tree with a Pidgey nest. Then we saw this HootHoot running out of the woods with an egg!"

"Who owns this HootHoot?" Officer Jenny asked. "This is a very serious charge."

"It's mine, but I know my HootHoot wouldn't steal an egg," Ralph said.

"He didn't," Ash cried. "In fact, your HootHoot was trying to save the egg. Derek's Sneasel is the egg thief! And I can prove it!"

What proof does Ash have? Do you know? Turn to the answer key to see if you are right.

Officer Jenny's Grid

Officer Jenny is on the trail of a Pokémon thief who has stolen two special Pokémon. You can help her find them! Follow the instructions below to cross out letters in the grid. The remaining letters will spell the names of the Pokémon.

1. Cross out any letters that appear in this Pokémon's name:
2. Cross out any letters that appear in this Pokémon's name:
3. Cross out the letter "T" for Thief.

A	E	U	S	M	R	P	A
K	I	E	T	O	L	K	R
T	N	L	Z	H	Z	T	M
A	T	Y	M	P	R	T	L
K	N	Z	T	O	M	U	I

— — — — — — and — — — — —

Poké Points: **total**

Answer Key

PAGES 3-4
MEMORY TEST 1
1. 2
2. 2
3. Wobbuffet
4. Meowth
5. Yes
6. Wobbuffet
7. James
8. R

PAGE 5
MISTY'S GRID
Kecleon and Wooper

PAGES 6-9
BATTLE BUSTERS 1
1. c) Raiku (Electric beats Poison/Flying)
2. a) Slugma (Fire beats Grass/Flying)
3. c) Pichu (Electric beats Water)
4. b) Sudowoodo (Rock beats Normal)
5. b) Azurill (Water beats Ground)
6. b) Remoraid (Water beats Grass)
7. c) Feraligatr (Water beats Fire/Rock)
8. a) Scizor (Bug/Steel beats Psychic)

PAGES 10–11
EARS TO YOU!

1. Gligar
2. Aipom
3. Azurill
4. Furret
5. Hoppip
6. Girafarig
7. Teddiursa
8. Ampharos
9. Elekid
10. Umbreon

PAGES 12–13
LOGIC PUZZLE 1

1. Ash won a HootHoot doll.
2. Misty won a Marill doll.
3. Brock won a Caterpie doll.
4. Tracey won a Politoed doll.

PAGES 14–15
ELECTRIC POKÉMON SEARCH

Ash knows the potion won't work because the "scientists" were lying. The scientist said he gave a Slugma two tablespoons of Pretty Pokémon Potion before bed, and after the Slugma slept all night, it woke up beautiful. Slugma don't sleep — they wouldn't be able to move if they stayed still for that long! After Ash pointed out this lie, the "scientists" tried to run away. Ash sent Pikachu after them, and after one of Pikachu's Thundershocks, their disguises fell off. It was Team Rocket, trying to trick people out of their money. The potion was just ordinary water.

PAGES 18–19
SECRET MESSAGE 1

We will get Natu and Cleffa.

PAGES 20–21
HIDDEN NAME CHALLENGE

1. Co*me w*ith me.
2. The s*hop pip*ed music over a loudspeaker.
3. Mom served me a go*od dish* of ice cream.
4. I've got *to get ice* for my water.
5. The white l*ab ra*ts chattered in their cage.
6. Please get the *horse a* drink.
7. Do you *see l*ights over there?
8. This new cleaner gets *grime r*ight off!

52

9. It is f**un own**ing a bike.
10. Mich**ele kid**s around a lot.
11. Most mice **fear ow**ls.
12. Close the window or el**se a dra**ft will get in.

PAGES 22–23
AMAZING ANAGRAMS
1. Ledian
2. Granbull
3. Bellossom
4. Hypno
5. Mantine
6. Meowth
7. Tangela
8. Crobat
9. Sentret
10. Skarmory

PAGE 24
NURSE JOY'S GRID
Bayleef and Girafarig

PAGES 25–26
MEMORY TEST 2
1. Pikachu
2. no
3. Noctowl
4. a Poké Ball
5. open

6. Phanpy
7. yes
8. standing

PAGES 27–29
WHO'S THAT CHARACTER?
1. Brock
2. Jessie
3. Todd
4. Nurse Joy
5. Misty
6. James
7. Professor Oak
8. Officer Jenny
9. Tracey
10. Giovanni
11. Liza
12. Gary
13. Sammy
14. Iron Mask

PAGES 30–32
BATTLE BUSTERS 2
1. b) Gligar (Ground/Flying beats Poison)
2. a) Cyndaquil (Fire beats Bug/Flying)
3. b) Flaafy (Electric beats Water/Poison)
4. c) Suicune (Water beats Fire)
5. c) Phanpy (Ground beats Electric)
6. a) Magby (Fire beats Bug)

7. b) Alakazam (Psychic beats Fighting)
8. a) Delibird (Ice beats Dragon)

PAGES 33–35
MINI-MYSTERY 2

Eric said that Ash had his Chikorita use Thundershock on Feraligatr. Chikorita is a Grass Pokémon, and it does not know any electric attacks. When faced with his lie, Eric admitted the truth. Ash was able to battle the Pokémon trainers at the gym.

PAGES 36–37
LOGIC PUZZLE 2

1. Pikachu became friends with Phanpy.
2. Bayleef became friends with Hoppip.
3. Totodile became friends with Magby.
4. Bulbasaur became friends with Eevee.
5. Cyndaquil became friends with Cubone.

PAGES 38–39
NORMAL POKÉMON SEARCH

PAGES 40-41
SWEET FEET

1. Shuckle
2. Sudowoodo
3. Spinarak
4. Octillery
5. Krabby
6. Murkrow
7. Natu
8. Bellsprout
9. Houndoom
10. Politoed

PAGES 42-43
SECRET MESSAGE 2

1. Celebi can travel through time.
2. Azurill will evolve into Marill.
3. Wailmer is a Whale Pokémon.
4. Kecleon can change color.
5. Suicune can clean polluted water.

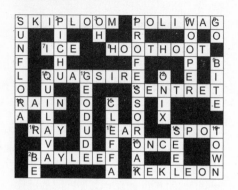

PAGES 47-48
MINI-MYSTERY 3

Not only are Sneasel notorious for stealing Pidgey eggs, but Derek said he followed a pair of footprints to the tree. HootHoot only hops on one leg. There would have been only one footprint leading to the tree. Officer Jenny went back to the tree, and the footprints matched Derek's Sneasel. HootHoot had grabbed the egg from the Sneasel to stop the Sharp Claw Pokémon from eating it.

PAGE 49
OFFICER JENNY'S GRID

Espeon and Hypno

Scoring Chart

Congratulations! You've finished all of the puzzles in the book. Take a minute to add up all of the Poké Points you've earned. Then look at the chart to compare your Pokémon knowledge with some of the characters in the Pokémon universe.

1–50 = Molly
When *Pokémon the Movie 2000* ended, little Molly was just learning how to be a Pokémon trainer. Like Molly, you are just beginning your journey. But keep at it — practice makes perfect!

51–100 = Team Rocket
If Team Rocket spent more time studying Pokémon than trying to steal them, they'd probably be a lot happier. Still, Jessie and James have done a pretty good job with Arbok and Weezing. Like Team Rocket, you know something about Pokémon — you just need to apply yourself!

101–150 = Ash and Misty
Ash and Misty have learned a lot since they began their journey — but they still have more to

learn. Like them, you love Pokémon and won't give up until you become a Pokémon Master!

151–200 = Brock

Brock's dream is to become a Pokémon breeder, and he spends most of his spare time learning all he can about Pokémon. Like Brock, you are almost a Pokémon pro. Younger trainers come to you when they need advice.

OVER 200 = Professor Oak

Good for you! Like Professor Oak, you are a certified Pokémon expert. Do you think they make a lab coat in your size?